Arthur E. Clarke

Letters Written During an European Tour

Arthur E. Clarke

Letters Written During an European Tour

ISBN/EAN: 9783337189877

Printed in Europe, USA, Canada, Australia, Japan

Cover: Foto ©Andreas Hilbeck / pixelio.de

More available books at **www.hansebooks.com**

LETTERS

WRITTEN DURING A

EUROPEAN TOUR

BY

ARTHUR E. CLARKE.

MANCHESTER, N. H.:
PRINTED FOR PRIVATE CIRCULATION.
1879.

PREFATORY.

THE following letters were written by my son, Arthur
Eastman Clarke, who was one of the party that visited
Europe under the guidance of Dr. Tourjee, in 1878.
They were originally written for and published in the "Mirror," on which he had been a reporter for two years previous,
and are reproduced in compliance with the request of many
personal friends, who desire them in a form more convenient
for reference and preservation.

JOHN B. CLARKE.

MANCHESTER, N. H., June, 1879.

LETTERS.

I.

THE educational party organized by Dr. Eben Tourjee, of Boston, Mass., which sailed from New York, Saturday, June 29, in the steamship "Devonia," of the Anchor line, arrived in this beautiful and picturesque city yesterday, late in the afternoon, having landed at Greenock early that morning and proceeded by special trains, carriages, and steamers, from there through the lake region to here.

Before speaking about what we have done since coming ashore, I will say a few words in regard to our voyage. We were fortunate in having delightful weather most of the way across, and the days passed away very quickly. After being four days out it came on rough, and the majority of the party succumbed to that much-to-be-dreaded ill, sea-sickness. A very few escaped it. As soon as the waves subsided, however, all was serene again, with a few exceptions, and the last forty-eight hours on the ocean saw everybody in the best of spirits, and those who had paid the most tribute to Neptune were the liveliest of us all. The party numbers two hundred and fifty, and the members come from many walks in life and represent nearly every State in the Union. It is the largest excursion party that ever went out from America. Our list includes men well known in the musical and literary world.

Nearly every evening of the trip over, an entertainment was held in the saloon of the vessel, which, for impromptu affairs, were the best of the kind I ever attended. No little artistic ability was manifested in some of the efforts essayed. The entertainments consisted chiefly of readings, vocal and instrumental music, burlesque acting, lectures, etc. Several original poems, written on board the ship, were delivered. One of these, by the Rev. C. H. Beale, of Centre Moriches, L. I., was particularly pleasing, being extremely bright.

Among the many ways in which the hours of the day were spent by the gentlemen was in playing "shuffle board," a game very extensively practised by sailors, and requiring considerable dexterity to succeed well at it. A steady eye and a strong wrist are necessary to play it well. I will not attempt a detailed description of it.

Of course a great deal of writing was done by members of the party. The majority of persons who go to Europe commence to keep a journal as soon as they step on the deck of the steamer that is to carry them over. I believe it is estimated that three-fourths of all who attempt to make a record of their doings and seeings while traveling in this country, signally fail to do so. Some drop off very quickly, others linger for a few weeks, but the few only succeed in the undertaking which is so fruitful of satisfaction and enjoyment when completed, but the production of which is attended with much hard labor. On board the "Devonia" there was the usual quota of journal-keepers. Quite a number have fallen by the wayside already, others show unmistakable signs of weariness in their well-doing, and the rest sharpen their pencils, when asked if they intend to keep up their writing during the entire trip, with an air which seems to say, "Keep it up? Do I look like a person who does anything by halves? You evidently are weak-minded. I always carry out whatever I undertake."

On the way over we fell in with a number of vessels bound for America, and the sight of them was like meeting an old acquaintance, bringing joy to every heart on board.

During the trip several incidents occurred worthy of special notice. One was the death and burial of a steerage passenger. and the other was the falling in with an English war fleet.

Both events created considerable excitement, especially the latter, as the fleet was met about midnight, and the captain, crew, and passengers were quite certain, judging from the movements of the vessels, that it was a Russian fleet. Arms were got in readiness, and every preparation for an encounter made. Our ship sailed a long distance out of her course in order to avoid the fleet, and when the captain saw he was not pursued, he signaled the admiral-ship, and, after giving the name of his steamer, received the information that the fleet was English, and bound in the direction of America. The fleet numbered seven iron-clads. A great feeling of relief filled the breasts of all on the "Devonia" when the nationality of the vessels was learned. The burial of the passenger who died was exceedingly solemn and impressive. It occurred Sunday noon, in the presence of nearly all the passengers and crew. The remains of the deceased were inclosed in a canvas bag, around which was placed the stars and stripes. The surgeon of the ship read the burial service, and when he came to "consign your body to the deep," the remains were cast into the sea, striking the water with a loud splash and instantly disappearing from sight. As the body slid off the deck of the ship the flag was removed. The board upon which the remains were placed after the death of the deceased, was thrown into the ocean, sailors being very superstitious about retaining anything which a dead body has touched.

The average distance made daily by the "Devonia" was about two hundred and eighty miles, but July 9 we went three hundred and seventeen miles. Land was first sighted Tuesday morning about nine o'clock, and a glimpse of *terra firma* once again was hailed with demonstrative manifestations of delight. It was the north coast of Ireland which we saw, and the captain very accommodatingly ran the steamer quite near the shore in order that we might obtain a good view of the country, which was beautiful in the extreme. Everything in the shape of vegetation was very luxuriant, and the dark, rich green of the verdure showed clearly why the "Emerald Isle" was thus christened. The fields were inclosed with high hedges of blackthorn, which added materially to their attractiveness, as did also the absence of stones and rocks on their surface.

We obtained a good view of that peculiar formation known as the "Giant's Causeway," pictures of which we remember to have first seen in an old geography. We will not enter into a description of it, as its structure is familiar to nearly everybody who ever attended school.

A portion of the coast which we passed was extremely rough and precipitous. Enormous caves penetrated far into the sides of the cliffs, and about the mouth hundreds of birds were flying. Many of the birds followed in the wake of our vessel for miles, picking up fragments of food which were thrown overboard.

Leaving the coast of Ireland we steered for Scotland, and ere long the land about which Scott has so graphically written, broke upon our vision. No wonder the inhabitants of this country deeply love their native land. It is a charming country, picturesque and inviting, with the most beautiful scenery and surroundings imaginable. And the atmosphere, — how invigorating and life-giving it is! It causes the blood to flow through the veins like the tingling air of a late fall morning in New Hampshire. The dwellings scattered along the shore were so romantically situated, and so novel and pleasing in architecture, that we gazed upon them in silent admiration. Now and then we would pass a small village, the buildings of which looked like toy houses. Occasionally a large and stately castle, standing upon a sightly eminence and surrounded by grounds most artistically laid out and beautified, would come into view. Among the most noticeable residences which were pointed out to us were those of the Duke of Hamilton, the Marquis of Lorne, and one owned by several gentlemen heavily interested in the Cunard line of steamers.

We sailed up the Frith of the Clyde late in the afternoon of Tuesday, and anchored off Greenock about ten o'clock in the evening. The following morning we went ashore early. It seemed very strange to be once more standing upon firm and unyielding earth, and at first the land appeared to be heaving and swelling like the sea. This illusion, however, quickly passed away. It was at Greenock that I obtained my first impression of English railroad trains. I had frequently read of them, but was not prepared to behold such comical-looking, dirty "coops." The cars are much smaller and lighter than those used in America, and are divided into compartments, each one of which accommodates six persons, who sit facing each other, three on a side. I was agreeably disappointed, when the train commenced to move, at the freedom from jar which was noticeable. I must say I never rode so comfortably for an hour in a train at home as I did during this my first trip in an English car. Subsequently I have learned that all the cars here are not such ill-looking, dirty things, as was the one I first sat in. Some of them are very elegantly painted and luxuriously upholstered. There are three classes of conveyances on every road; and the third class being for the poor people, a very small price is charged for riding in them.

Glasgow is about an hour's travel from Greenock. We did not stop in this city, so famous for its shipping, but, changing cars, pushed on to Edinburgh by the way of the lakes. The ride through the Trossachs by carriage was delightful. We rode in high vehicles that resemble jaunting-cars in style, but are considerably larger; and the spirited horses attached to them whirled us along through a region charmingly picturesque and replete with romance.

Arriving at Loch Katrine we embarked on the steamer "Rob Roy," and for an hour enjoyed a sail on its waters. Leaving the steamer at Stronachlachar, we went by coach to Inversnaid, where we dined at one of those fine mountain hotels where everything that is served is so delicious. Subsequently we enjoyed a twenty-mile sail on that famous and lovely Scottish sheet of water of whose beauty poets have so often sung, — Loch Lomond. Its praise has not been sounded too highly. It merits all that has ever been said of it, and volumes would be required to contain this. Situated in a valley, surrounded on all sides by high hills and mountains, dotted with islands, its shores studded with beautiful residences, it is indeed an ideal spot, delightfully romantic.

It is needless to say that the sail on Loch Lomond was fruitful of exquisite pleasure. We left the steamer at Balloch Pier, and seated ourselves in the train for Edinburgh, which we reached about half-past six o'clock. I will not speak of the ride by rail from Greenock to Edinburgh, of the surprises that constantly unfolded themselves, but will only say that the objects passed, the towns gone through, abounded in interest, and we gazed upon the rapidly changing scenes with unalloyed pleasure. Two nights and a day were given us in the famous city of Edinburgh, the capital of Scotland, which is situated on a cluster of eminences a mile and a half south of the Frith of Forth — an arm of the sea which is here about six miles in breadth. The country around Edinburgh is a happy blending of hill and plain. The fields are very fertile, well cultivated, and ornamented with gardens and villas. Twelve hundred years ago, Edwin, a king of Northumbria, built a fort on the rocky height on which the castle of Edinburgh now stands, and hence, as is alleged, arose the name of Edwinsburgh, or Edinburgh. The population of Edinburgh, with its suburbs, is estimated at two hundred and sixty thousand. It abounds in places of interest, the principal of which our party visited, in the charge of old and experienced guides. A bird's-eye view of Edinburgh, to any one who has even a smattering of geology, suggests at once the primeval means by which it has become so picturesque. The first place a stranger usually goes to is the castle, which is replete with interest and romance. The castle is an immense stone structure, situated upon a rock three hundred and eighty-three feet above the level of the sea, and its battlements towering above the city may be seen in some directions for fifty miles. The rock is very precipitous on all sides but the east, and before the invention of artillery it must have been impregnable. In the southeast corner of the castle, is an old palace built by Queen Mary in 1565. On approaching the castle from the only accessible side, the Half-Moon Battery first strikes the eye. Salutes are fired from this battery on royal holidays and occasions of national rejoicing; and daily, at one o'clock, the time gun is fired from the same platform, by a wire stretching over the city from the Royal Observatory on Calton Hill. On the top of this observatory is a large ball which falls at one o'clock, Greenwich time, thus completing the connection of an electric current and discharging the gun.

The working of the time ball on the Equitable building in Boston, is, I believe, taken from the one here. I cannot enter into a detailed account of what we saw at the castle and else-where, as too much space would be required for that end.

The regalia and crown jewels in use by the Scottish sove-reigns previous to the Union were seen by us. They are very rich and elegant, and of almost priceless value, — diamonds, pearls, and rubies entering largely into their composition. The jewels were securely inclosed in a kind of cage of upright iron bars, and guarded by an officer. These jewels were lost once, for about a dozen years, and it was through the instrumentality of Sir Walter Scott that they were recovered. He instituted a search in a certain part of the castle, and found them buried many feet in the solid wall.

We went into the room in which Queen Mary gave birth to James VI., on the 19th of June, 1566; also Queen Margaret's chapel. The latter is a small building on the highest platform of the castle rock. The pious queen of Malcolm Canmore prob-ably built the chapel, and certainly worshiped in it during her residence in the castle till her death in 1093. Beside the chapel is "Mons Meg," an enormous gun, supposed to have been built under the direction of James IV., who in 1498 employed it at the siege of Nordham Castle. It was rent in 1680 when firing a salute, since which time it has been useless. The balls which were fired in it were large stones of about two and one-fourth feet diameter. Some of these are now piled alongside of Meg. The castle is now occupied by soldiers, a large portion of it being used for barracks. Whenever the Queen visits Edinburgh she makes her headquarters here, but that is not often. A Scotchman informed me that during the last ten years she had only been there three times.

In the arsenal there are thirty thousand stand of arms. Edin-burgh Castle is one of the forts enjoined by the treaty of Union to be kept up in Scotland. The view obtainable from the castle is magnificent.

The palace of Holyrood is another object of great interest. It is situated about a mile from the castle, and its site is not at all elevated.

The palace was built in connection with an abbey founded by David I., and this old structure was considerably renovated by James V. The whole, however, was destroyed by Cromwell, excepting the northwest angle of the building, Queen Mary's private apartments. All the rest is comparatively modern, having been built in the reign of Charles II., but in a way to harmonize with the older part then remaining. The architect on this occasion was Sir William Bruce.

Ascending a stone staircase from the piazza of the court, under the guidance of an attendant, we reach Queen Mary's rooms, so full of historical associations, and are naturally surprised to observe how simply the beautiful queen was accommodated. In the first place there is a vestibule where the blood of Rizzio is still shown upon the floor. Next is her presence chamber, — a room of large dimensions, with a carved oak roof embellished with ciphers of different kings, queens, and princes in faded paint and gold. The walls are decked with a great variety of pictures and prints, and some old chairs and other furniture are preserved. Adjacent to this apartment, occupying the front of the tower, is the bed-chamber of Mary, in which her bed is seen in a very decayed condition. The only other two apartments are a small dressing-room and a cabinet, in which last she was sitting, at supper, when Rizzio was assailed by his assassins conducted by Lord Darnley, Mary's husband. These two rooms contain a few objects of interest said to have belonged to the queen's toilet; also some tapestry wrought by her own hand.

Cold and deserted, and with all around having the appearance of age and decay, Mary's apartments cannot fail to inspire melancholy reflections; but to the reader of history the view of the scene here disclosed will at the same time afford a new pleasure — the satisfaction of seeing the actual spot where events took place which have for centuries been the theme of narratives and discussions. Having seen Mary's apartments, little else in the palace is worth looking at. In a long apartment in which takes place the election of representative Scottish peers for the House of Lords, are exhibited "portraits of a hundred and six Scottish monarchs." Being merely daubs with a fictitious likeness, they are treated with deserved contempt. The other apartments are fitted up principally in a modern style, for the accommodation of Queen Victoria and her royal consort.

I intended to have spoken of quite a number of other historic places visited in Edinburgh, but will leave them until another time, as I have already spun this letter to very great length.

II.

MY last letter was brought to a close before I had fin-
ished with the attractions of Edinburgh, and now I
will briefly allude to other objects of interest which
came under our observation.

St. Giles' Church is a large and conspicuous edifice of un-
known antiquity. Until the Reformation it was a collegiate
church, dedicated to St. Giles, the patron saint of the town. It
was provided with thirty-six altars, and had nearly one hundred
clergymen and other attendants. At the Reformation all this
was swept away, and for a while its ministrations were conducted by John Knox, the eminent Scotch reformer. The
church is a massive structure, and now three separate services
are held in it at the same time on Sundays. In the tower is a
chime of bells which are played daily at one o'clock.

Near St. Giles' is John Knox's house. It is shown for a small
fee, and is well worth seeing. The house is in a good state
of preservation. Over the door is the inscription, "Lufe God
abuf all, and ye nychtbour as yiself." The window from which
Knox addressed the multitude was looked out of by us with
peculiar interest. The great reformer died here in the sixty-
seventh year of his age, November 24, 1572. I forgot to say that
it was in St. Giles' Church, on the memorable day in 1637 when
the obnoxious liturgy of Laud was to be introduced into Scotland by authority, that Jennie Geddes threw her stool at the
head of the dean. The famous stool is preserved in the Anti-
quarian Museum. It was well for the dean that the stool
missed its mark, as it is very heavy.

In an old churchyard which we visited, lie the remains of
Robert Ferguson, Adam Smith, and Dugald Stewart. It is said

that when Burns visited this churchyard in 1786 he was moved to tears.

The national monument, situated on the summit of Calton Hill, a high elevation from which a commanding view can be obtained, is a memorial of the gallant officers and men who fell at Waterloo. It was projected in 1816, and the idea was to reproduce an exact model of the Parthenon at Athens. The project was received with such enthusiasm that £6,000, about $30,000, was subscribed at the first public meeting held for its promotion. Various circumstances occurred to chill the patriotic ardor, and the monument has never been finished, and probably no addition will ever be made to it. The foundation stone was laid in 1822, and the entire amount subscribed was spent in the erection of three colossal steps and twelve columns. Various proposals have been made for the completion of the design, but they have not come to any practical issue. Many persons are of the opinion that, as a matter of taste, the monument is more picturesque as it stands. There are two other monuments on Calton Hill: one erected to Dugald Stewart, professor of mathematics and moral philosophy in the Edinburgh University, and the other to the memory of John Playfair, professor of mathematics at the same institution.

The Scott monument on Prince street is one of the grandest ornaments in the city. It was erected in 1844, at an expense of £16,154, from designs furnished by George Kemp, a young, self-taught architect of great promise, who did not live to see the work completed.

The monument is an open Gothic cross or tower, two hundred feet high, covering at its base a marble statue of Sir Walter and his favorite dog. Many of the niches in the monument are occupied by statues of the most familiar characters in Scott's novels and poems, and a Scott museum is in process of formation in an apartment immediately above the great central arch. The monument fronts the house in which David Hume, the historian, died. The monument is viewed by all strangers as a model of art. There are many other objects of attraction in this city, but I will not speak of any more.

The city is very beautifully laid out, and is a model of cleanliness. Its streets are broad, and a number of lovely public gardens add to its attractiveness very considerably. One is immediately struck, upon his arrival in Edinburgh, with the politeness of the inhabitants. They will impart any amount of information in the most courteous manner. In fact, that trait has been noticeable in all the people with whom I have come in contact. There is no night in this city at this season of the year, the sun rising at three o'clock and setting about nine. The intervening hours are twilight. Fine print can be read in the street at half-past ten o'clock.

Six months from now, the state of affairs will be exactly the reverse, and darkness will prevail. The night of my arrival I visited a floral and fruit exhibition in a large coliseum, which surpassed anything of the kind I ever beheld. Roses of innumerable varieties, and measuring two feet in circumference, were to be seen, also strawberries as large as a good-sized russet apple, and flowers and plants of rare fragrance and luxuriance. Among other things on exhibition were a lot of cucumbers, of about the diameter of those usually seen in Manchester, but of a prodigious length, some of them measuring four feet. Nearly everything shown was much larger than what is grown in New England. Several thousand people were inside the vast building when I was there, and the scene, enlivened by music from two bands, was gay in the extreme.

I was surprised to ascertain what an enormous number of Scott's books are published in this city every year. Editions in every conceivable style are issued. Year after year the never-tiring press throws off the same sheets, and yet the public are unsatisfied, and call for more.

The party left Edinburgh Friday morning for London, stopping on the way at Melrose Abbey and Abbotsford. Melrose is thirty-five miles from Edinburgh, and upon our arrival there we seated ourselves in large carriages and were driven to the house of Sir Walter Scott, about three miles from the station. It is a curious structure, half country-seat, half castle. Its location and surroundings are noticeably beautiful and romantic. The house is a perfect museum of curiosities and relics identified with Scottish history. It is said that Scott was led to select this site for his residence because it made him owner of the whole ground of the famous border battle of Melrose. The building of the house was begun in 1811, and was gradually extended year after year, till it attained dimensions considerably beyond what had been first contemplated. On the mansion and estate at least £50,000 were expended. The property is now owned by Mr. Hope Scott, a relative of the novelist. The walls of the house, as well as those of the garden, are set with curious old sculptured stones gathered from ancient buildings and ruins in all parts of Scotland. The grounds are beautifully laid out in terraces and winding paths, and rustic seats and lounges are placed wherever the view is specially interesting or striking. The library is the largest and most magnificent of all the rooms in the house, being sixty feet long by fifty broad. The top is elaborately carved after old Gothic models, and the walls are covered with bookcases containing nearly twenty thousand volumes.

The small room Sir Walter used as his study, and which is most identified with his renown as the Great Magician of the North, is entered from the library. It is a small apartment, lighted by a single window. Scott's writing-table, the black leather arm-chair he used, and one other chair are all the movable furniture it contains. In a glass case the clothes worn by Sir Walter immediately before his death are carefully preserved. These consist of a blue coat with large brass buttons, plaid trousers, a broad-brimmed, light, tall hat, and a pair of stout shoes; his walking-stick is laid beside them.

The rooms of the house are overflowing with curiosities, among which we saw the musket of that redoubtable outlaw, Rob Roy, a pair of pistols found in Napoleon's carriage at the battle of Waterloo, a silver urn presented by Lord Byron, a snuff-box studded with large diamonds, formerly owned by George IV., and a piece of Robert Bruce's coffin. There were, among the many things upon the walls, several complete suits of tilting armor, stout old battle-axes, English steel maces, and other weapons, many with histories and from bloody fields whose horrors are a prominent feature on the pages of history. Among the more striking pictures upon the walls of the different rooms was the portrait of the head of Mary Queen of Scots, upon a charger, said to have been taken a few hours after her execution. Then there were the stern, heavily-molded features of Cromwell, Charles XII., and Charles II., and a collection of original etchings by Turner and other artists, the designs for the "Provincial Antiquities of Scotland."

In the grounds about the house are the most beautiful and luxuriant ivies growing that I ever saw.

Bidding adieu to Abbotsford, we visited Melrose Abbey, situated only a few minutes' walk from Melrose station. Melrose Abbey, taking it altogether, and comparing it with any other ancient building which remains in Scotland, is admittedly the finest example of Gothic architecture and sculpture in the country. It was here that the architect of the Edinburgh Scott monument, and many other architects of reputation, drank in the inspiration which has done so much to revive in modern times a taste for this style of architecture.

Melrose Abbey was founded by David I. The monks first settled here were a community of the Cistercian order. They were given to agricultural and pastoral pursuits, and their primitive mode of life was simple and frugal. In course of time their manners degenerated, so that, as the old ballad says : —

> " The monks of Melrose made fat kail
> On Fridays, when they fasted,
> And wanted neither beef nor ale
> As long's their neighbors' lasted."

The monastery was founded in 1136, and was ten years in building. In 1322 it was destroyed by the English, and rebuilt with two thousand pounds sterling, given by Robert Bruce, a sum equal to about fifty thousand pounds at the present time.

In 1385, 1544, twice in 1546, and once in 1569 the abbey was partially laid in ruins. The abbey is now the property of the Duke of Buccleuch. Truly this is a glorious old structure, and one cannot fail to admire it. The blue arch of the heavens is now its only roof, and from its shattered walls, overrun with ivy, noisy rooks fly hither and thither, keeping up a continual chatter.

But the majestic sweep of the great Gothic arches, the superb columns, and the innumerable elegant carvings on every side, the graves of monarchs, knights, and wizards, marked with their quaint, antique inscriptions, — all form a scene of most charming and beautiful effects. These ruins have furnished material for the erecting of a town prison, and also for other buildings.

The grandest object, whether seen from without or within, is the great east window, thirty-seven feet high and sixteen broad. The beauty of its tracery is singularly delicate and striking. Here, buried in the abbey, are many kings and illustrious personages. Here is the spot where Robert Bruce's heart was buried; here is the grave of the Earl of Douglas. It is said that Alexander II., king of Scotland, lies buried at the high altar. A flat, mossy stone, broken across the middle, is reputed to be the grave of the famous wizard, or natural philosopher, Michael Scott, whose magic books were interred with him. In "The Lay of the Last Minstrel" his funeral is spoken of in weird terms. What the abbey must have been when it was fresh from the workmen's hands, we can hardly imagine, but that it was wondrously beautiful is evident. Days could be most profitably spent in the abbey, and the few hours we were there were too short to fully appreciate all the beauties to be seen.

After leaving Melrose we went on, with a few stops, to London, which we reached late in the evening. The large size of the party necessitated its being divided into two sections, one section quartering at the Grand Midland Hotel, and the other at the Inns of Court. Both are very large houses, the former being one of the grandest in London.

Our stay in this city was limited to five days. What we saw there I will refer to in my next letter.

III.

HEIDELBERG, GERMANY, July 25, 1878.

IT is of London that I am to speak chiefly in this letter, and the magnitude of the subject almost staggers me. Necessarily the descriptions of what I saw here must be brief, but volumes could be easily written of the vast number of interesting objects which this great metropolis and its environs contain, and which every American who goes to London should visit. Our party remained here about five days, and *did* the city pretty thoroughly. Traveling as we do, — all our wants and requirements in the shape of carriages, rooms, meals, etc., being anticipated, — we do not experience any of the annoyances incident to journeying otherwise. Consequently, on reaching London at ten o'clock in the evening, we did not have to stretch out a finger to help ourselves, but got into the long line of carriages that were waiting for us, and were quickly driven to our hotel. We stopped at the Midland Grand and Inns of Court hotels, two of the best in the city. As the list of the names of our party had been sent on in advance, our rooms were ready for us as soon as we reached the hotel, and, after indulging in a bountiful supper, we repaired to them to secure rest and strength to fortify us for five days of London sight-seeing. To illustrate the manner in which our party is cared for as regards luggage (the English never say baggage), I will say that our trunks, which we left on the steamer at Greenock Wednesday morning, were found in our rooms, all unstrapped, awaiting our arrival at the hotels in London.

Without mentioning the order in which we visited the different places of interest, I will confine myself to giving a brief description of each, also of the manners and customs of our English brethren as they appeared to me.

WESTMINSTER ABBEY.

Every student of history is more or less familiar with Westminster Abbey, and it is so fraught with historic interest as to be worth a journey across the ocean to see; the last resting-place of kings, queens, princes, poets, sculptors, and divines, who are now slumbering side by side, laid low by the great leveler Death. The abbey is an immense structure, and its great age is evident in nearly everything about it, except the guides. In form, it is the usual long cross, and has three entrances. Its greatest length is about four hundred feet, and two of its towers rise to the height of two hundred and twenty-five feet. After entering the abbey, turn whichever way you will, you are constantly reminded that England's choicest dust rests here, for innumerable memorials are to be seen on every hand, marking the spot where remains are buried. Portions of the abbey are set apart into what are called chapels, in which tombs have been erected. The oldest of the chapels is that of St. Edward the Confessor. It contains, besides the monument to its founder, those of many other monarchs. The most elegant tomb-chapel is that of Henry VII. It is most exquisitely carved on every side. Here is the tomb of Edward III., who died in 1377. Upon it rests his effigy, with the shield and sword which he carried in France, — a big, two-handled affair, seven feet long, and weighing eighteen pounds. In one chapel is a beautiful tomb erected to Mary Queen of Scots, and near it is another erected by King James I. to Queen Elizabeth, bearing the recumbent effigy of that sovereign, supported by four lions. Queen Mary ("Bloody Mary"), who burned about seventy persons a year at the stake during four years of her reign, rests here in the same vault. The nine chapels of the abbey are crowded with the tombs and monuments of kings and others of royal birth down to the time of George II., when Windsor Castle was made the repository of the royal remains.

Besides monuments to royal personages, I noticed those of men who have, by great deeds, and gifts of great inventions to mankind, achieved names that will outlive many of royal blood.

In the chapel of St. Paul there is a colossal figure of James Watt, who so developed the wonderful power of steam. There is also a tablet to Sir Humphrey Davy, and in the same chapel is a full-length statue of Mrs. Siddons, the tragic actress.

One wonderfully executed monumental group which attracted my attention, and which is greatly admired by visitors generally, represented a tomb, from the half-opened marble doors of which a figure of Death has just issued, and is in the very act of casting his dart at a lady who is sinking, affrighted, into the arms of her husband, who is rising, startled from his seat upon the top of the tomb. The group is terribly realistic, and the expression of affright of the two figures is wonderful, while Death, with the shroud half falling off, revealing the fleshless ribs, skull, and bones of the full-length skeleton, is something little short of appalling in its marvelous execution.

Many a royal person lies in the abbey without a stone to mark his resting-place. Among these is the grave of the merry monarch, Charles II. The time I spent in the abbey was all too short to study the elaborate and splendid works of sculpture, the curious inscriptions, and the noteworthy appendages. Days might be advantageously passed here. Nearly every American who visits the abbey inquires for the " Poet's Corner," and here I took special delight in lingering. Here we find the brightest names in English literature recorded. One is surrounded by names of those that the world has delighted to honor. Here is a medallion portrait of Ben Jonson, who died in 1627, with the well-known inscription below, —

" O rare Ben Jonson."

There is a bust of Butler, author of " Hudibras," and here is a tablet marking the resting-place of Spenser, author of the " Faerie Queene," and near at hand is a bust of Milton. The spot where lies Geoffrey Chaucer, the father of English poetry and author of the " Canterbury Tales," is marked by a tomb with a carved Gothic canopy above it.

The grave of the immortal Shakespeare is, of course, looked upon with peculiar interest. The place is designated by a statue of the great dramatist, leaning upon a pile of books resting upon a pedestal, and supporting a scroll upon which are inscribed lines from his play of "The Tempest." Upon the base of the pillar upon which the statue leans, are the sculptured heads of Henry V., Richard II., and Queen Elizabeth.

Gray's monument is a Cupid unveiling a medallion of the poet. A large marble monument to Handel represents the great musician playing. There are a host of other monuments, tablets, and bas-reliefs to heroes, scholars, professors, actors, and writers, but I will mention only one other, which always attracts the attention of Americans. It is a bas-relief representing the flag of truce conveyed to General Washington, asking the life of Major Andre. Over this group Britannia is represented weeping.

ST. PAUL'S.

From almost any point in London the dome of St. Paul's can be seen. The church is located in the oldest and most crowded part of the city. All around it are names with which for years we have all been familiar. Newgate, where the old walls of London stood, is near at hand, as are also Ludgate Hill, Fleet Street, the Old Bailey, and Cheapside. St. Paul's is built of what is called Portland stone, originally light colored, but now grimed and blackened with smoke and age. The length of the building is five hundred feet; its breadth two hundred and eighty feet; and the top of the cross on the dome is three hundred and sixty feet from the sidewalk. The edifice covers two acres of ground. St. Paul's is replete with interest. It was built by Sir Christopher Wren. The corner-stone of it was laid in 1675, and thirty-five years were required for its completion.

There are over fifty splendid monuments in St. Paul's, and many of them are very elaborate and elegant affairs. The most noteworthy ones are those erected to the memory of Lord Nelson and the Duke of Wellington. The former is a splendid black marble sarcophagus. It was originally built for Cardinal Wolsey. The Duke of Wellington's sarcophagus is of porphyry, and the inclosure about it is lighted with gas from granite candelabra.

In other parts of the church are slabs denoting the resting-places of men well known to the world. Among them we notice those of Sir Joshua·Reynolds, the great painter, Dr. Samuel Johnson, Henry Hallam, Sir John Moore, and Sir Henry Lawrence, who died defending Lucknow in 1857.

Among the many interesting places in St. Paul's is the Whispering Gallery. This is reached by a flight of two hundred and sixty steps, and about half way to it is the church library, containing many rare and curious works, among which is the first Book of Common Prayer ever printed. The Whispering Gallery extends for a distance of one hundred and forty yards, and whispered conversation can be carried on between persons seated at the extreme opposite sides of the space. The clapping of hands gives out a report almost as sharp as the discharge of a pistol. The Geometrical Stairs are a flight of ninety steps near the library, so ingeniously constructed that they all hang together without any visible means of support except the bottom step.

The clock of St. Paul's is a gigantic timepiece, indeed, when you get up to it. Its faces are fifty-seven feet in circumference, and the minute-hand a huge bar of steel, weighing seventy-five pounds, and nearly ten feet in length. The *little* hand is six feet long, and weighs forty-four pounds. The figures on the dial are over two feet in length.

Above the Whispering Gallery are the Stone and Golden Galleries, from which magnificent views are obtainable. Next comes an ascent into the ball, which, together with the cross, fifteen feet high, is upheld by a series of huge iron bars. Steps are notched into these bars, so that the ascent is easily made. Looking down from this great elevation, pedestrians upon the street look like Lilliputians, and unless one's head is exceedingly clear it will reel at the sight. Although the globe looks very small from the ground, yet a dozen men can stand in it. I suppose the twin sight to St. Paul's Church is London Tower, so we will next visit that.

THE TOWER OF LONDON.

Here we are in the Tower of London; in a structure which has figured most prominently in the history of the past. Every part of it is replete with thrilling story. It has witnessed some of the blackest and foulest deeds that ever were chronicled. Its foundation dates back to Cæsar's time, and the scenes which have occurred within its walls invest it with more historic interest than any other European palace or prison. Shakespeare has made this Tower to play a prominent and a bloody part in his dramas, and as we walk about in it we can almost fancy we see some of the characters he has so vividly drawn, and hear the cries of some of the victims who have died here. The Tower covers no less than thirteen acres, and inside the inclosure there are fourteen towers; namely, the Bell Tower, White, Bloody, Beauchamp, Flint, Devereux, Brick, Record, Bowyer, Jewel, Constable, Broad, Arrow, and Salt.

The guides to the Tower are attired in the costume of the yeomen of the guard of Henry the Eighth's time, and they are principally old soldiers who receive the position as a reward for bravery or faithful service. The admission to the Tower is sixpence, and an additional sixpence is charged to see the crown jewels. One of the first interesting features is the armory, where thousands and thousands of weapons — pistols, swords, cutlasses, and bayonets — are kept, enough to equip a large army. Beauchamp Tower has much to attract, for here we began to visit the prisons of many an unhappy and unfortunate captive. The walls bear many inscriptions, which those who were confined there made. In one room is the word "Jane" cut, which is said to refer to Lady Jane Grey. The autograph of Philip Howard, Earl of Arundel, who was beheaded in 1572 for aspiring to the hand of Mary Queen of Scots, is to be seen over a fireplace.

In the White Tower is a small room, where Sir Walter Raleigh wrote his "History of the World." Near by is the block and the executioner's ax, which, in Elizabeth's reign, severed Essex's head from his body. The walls of this tower are about fifteen feet thick. The Bloody Tower is examined with the most interest, for the stones in it are red with the blood of many victims, and the walls seem to cry out in tones of horror at the deeds of violence that have been enacted within them. In a small cell, ten feet high and four feet deep, we are told Guy Fawkes was confined three days, which seems incredible to believe, as the only air which can get into it comes through the key-hole of the door. Tower Green is a small square, railed with iron, on which stood the scaffold where Anne Boleyn was executed. Here, also, Lady Jane Grey poured forth her blood, and the Countess of Salisbury, aged seventy years, was killed by order of Henry VIII.

It was in this tower that Clarence was drowned in the butt of Malmsey; and William Wallace, Lord Bacon, Cranmer, and Latimer were imprisoned here. But it is needless to further catalogue the names and deeds associated with this structure. The bloody tales are told in history.

The Jewel Tower is eagerly sought by Americans, and it is amusing to notice the awe akin to reverence with which they look upon the glittering emblems of royalty kept here. The jewels, of course, are worth a king's ransom, are indeed elegant, and have adorned many a royal head; but these are insufficient reasons why so many of our people should regard them, apparently, with veneration. Diamonds, emeralds, pearls, and other precious stones enter lavishly into the structure of the crown and royal scepter. The display here reminds one of an immense jewelry store, and the blaze of light which the stones emit is almost dazzling.

The visit to the Tower was attended with much pleasure, and a full description of what is to be seen here would fill a good-sized volume.

I had hoped to finish the attractions in London in a single letter, but find that I have already spun this out to rather a tedious length, so will lay by my pen for the present.

IV.

BIDDING adieu to London, we proceeded by rail to Queenborough, and took the steamer for Flushing, which was reached after an all-night ride upon the English Channel and the North Sea. Here our baggage was examined, but the detention was very short, and soon a train was whirling us on to Antwerp through a most beautiful country, level as a prairie and in the highest state of cultivation. As new scenes were constantly unfolding themselves, the few hours of the journey sped by rapidly, freighted with interest. The country through which we passed, for a great part of the way, is covered with dikes, — huge embankments constructed to prevent the encroachment of the sea. The labor that was required to throw up these immense fortifications must have been enormous.

To strengthen the dikes, large numbers of trees are planted near them, the roots of which bind the earth very firmly. A curious feature about these trees is, that they are nearly all the same height, about seventy-five feet. As far as the eye can reach, the treetops are on a level. This is undoubtedly due to uniform and constant trimming for years after the trees are set out.

We were all of us struck with the exceeding fertility of the land, which was evident from the magnificent fields of grain and vegetables to be seen extending for miles and miles. It is the dry season now, and vegetation fairly jumps from the ground, which is in perfect condition for providing crops with necessary sustenance, made so by months of constant rain. As soon as one crop is harvested another is immediately planted, and the time required for the ripening of both is only about as long as it takes in New Hampshire for a single crop to attain maturity.

The women seem to do the greater part of the work in this country, and the fields swarm with them, busy with the sickle, rake, and hoe. No fences are to be seen here, as indeed is the case all over Europe, but for them there are various substitutes. In Holland and Belgium, rows of tall trees are most frequently used to mark the land boundaries, and ditches are also made to answer the same purpose; and these last serve an additional end by acting as reservoirs for water by which the soil is kept moist.

At last Antwerp is reached, and, as we were conveyed in carriages from the depot to Hotel de la Paix, we saw many curious sights in the way of buildings, people, equipages, etc.

We passed through the market square, which was filled with bare-headed, quaint-head-dressed women and curiously-attired peasants, arranging their vegetables, fruit, etc., and the air was filled with a perfect babel of voices. Dogs are made to do service in Holland, Belgium, and Germany, to a great extent, being harnessed to carts which hold several bushels. The animals are chiefly mastiffs, and are so admirably trained to the business, that, when attached to the cart, nothing will attract their attention from duty; and during the absence of their master or mistress they keep faithful watch and guard over the wagon and its contents.

Antwerp is a city of considerable commercial importance, as is evident from its splendid docks, two of which were built by Bonaparte, the walls of which are five feet thick. One of the dry docks here is the largest in Europe, being five hundred feet long, and capable of holding two ships of one thousand tons register each at a time.

Antwerp rejoices in a magnificent cathedral, which rises to a height of over four hundred feet. The exterior, although bearing unmistakable signs of age, is covered with architectural designs truly beautiful. The interior of the cathedral is grand and imposing; and the sculpturing and works of art to be seen are viewed with admiration by visitors. But the chief attraction here is a large collection of Rubens' best paintings, effectively arranged upon the walls of the cathedral. Everybody knows of the position which Rubens occupied in art; that he is one of the grand old masters whose pictures are most extensively copied. He lived and died here at Antwerp, and the old city is justly proud of her talented son. The Elevation and Descent from the Cross are considered the most remarkable of Rubens' works, and those we saw in the cathedral. The figures are portrayed with wonderful and faithful accuracy ; and, as we look, it seems to us as though their creator must have been inspired, to produce such life-like realizations with mere paint and brush.

In the church of St. Jacques is the tomb of Rubens, where are also more of his pictures, including his Holy Family.

The zoölogical gardens of Antwerp are very large and beautifully laid out, and the collection of wild animals is quite extensive. In the center of the grounds is a handsome stand, in which a band plays choice music every evening, when hundreds of the inhabitants come to stroll about and sit beneath the shade trees, and eat ices and drink light wines and beer, and smoke pipes and cigars.

Brussels was the next city we stopped at after leaving Antwerp, and here a sojourn of several days was made. We are in the lace country now, and the manufactories are one of the principal attractions here. Brussels, or Bruxelles, as the natives spell it, is a clean-looking city, and contains very many things of interest to the traveler. It is divided into two parts, the upper and lower city. The latter is crowded, and inhabited principally by the poorer and laboring classes, and contains many of the quaint, old-fashioned Dutch buildings of three centuries ago. The upper part of the city, where dwell the richer classes, contains fine, large, open squares and street-gardens, etc. We visited a museum at Brussels which contains some very fine pictures by Rubens, and a great many from the brush of an artist named Wiertz. Many of the subjects chosen by the latter were very singular and grotesque. One of the most horrible of the pictures represented a maniac mother, in a dimly-lighted room, cutting up one of her children with a butcher-knife, and putting the pieces into a pot boiling upon the fire. Every keyhole and crevice in the room is carefully covered, and the spectator seems to be getting a view from an unobserved crevice. The spectacle is a frightful one, being terribly realistic. The picture is viewed through a small aperture in a wall. The power of Wiertz at deception on canvas was wonderful. Many of his pictures cheat the observer most successfully, as, for instance, a painting of a table bearing an easel and some brushes, is usually taken for the real article, and people very often reach out their hands to take up one of the brushes. A very interesting church in Brussels is the splendid cathedral of St. Gudule, founded in 1010, the principal wonders of which are its magnificently painted windows and the pulpit, which is a wonder of the carver's art, and represents the expulsion of Adam and Eve from the Garden of Eden.

We went to one of the lace establishments here, and, of course, like everybody else, were surprised at the smallness of the buildings in which the business is carried on. The one I visited did not differ, externally, in the least from hundreds of mansions in the city, and a stranger would invariably take it for a private dwelling. The inside of the rooms I found to be rather small, and in each sat half a dozen women busily engaged in the manufacture of different kinds of lace.

Lace-making looks very simple, but it is a most laborious occupation, and requires the constant attention of those who are engaged in it. The thread of which the lace is constructed is wound on a score of long and slender spools, and it is by the lifting and moving of these spools that the different patterns are wrought. The pattern is marked with a pencil on a piece of paper, and lies on a wooden stand in front of the operative. When I saw the women lifting these spools, which they do with great rapidity, I thought they were simply getting their tools in order previous to commencing work; but as they did not change their mode of operation while I was there, it was evident that those were the maneuvers which they went through to make the lace. The lady in charge showed us many of her lace treasures, some of which were valued at hundreds of dollars. I saw some point-lace, most beautiful in design and exquisite in text-ure, resembling, more than anything else, a mass of spider's web. The women who are employed in these lace manufac-tories are very poorly paid, the most expert receiving only about twenty-five cents per day, and after a few years of labor they have to abandon it for something else, on account of failing eyesight.

Although, in Holland and Belgium, Dutch is the national lan-guage, nearly everybody speaks French, and in the principal hotels and places of business English-speaking persons are to be found, and the number of these is increasing yearly, owing to the thousands of Americans and English who each summer travel on the continent.

The principal attraction at Brussels is the field of the battle of Waterloo, situated about a dozen miles out of the city, and accessible by cars, or by a carriage-drive through a beautiful country on a smooth and well-kept road. The field is a large plain, intersected by several broad roads. Monuments rise here and there to mark the spots where the fight raged the hottest.

Here is a low ridge where Wellington's men lay until the Old Guard was almost upon them; then, rising at the word of com-mand, they poured their leaden hail into the breasts of the foe with frightful effect. We come to the chateau of Hougoumont, which sustained such a succession of desperate attacks. At the time of the battle the place was a gentleman's country-seat, and the shattered ruins of the buildings are highly interesting as reminders of the battle. Four companies of the English held this place for seven hours against an assaulting army, fifteen hundred members of which fell in less than an hour. Victor Hugo, in his "Les Miserables," describes this portion of the battle-field most vividly. Going into the orchard, we are shown where distinguished officers fell, and where Napoleon and Wel-lington directed the struggle. Marks made by bullets, axes, and flame, are distinctly visible in the ruins on the field, and give unmistakable evidence of the bloody struggle that history so thrillingly pictures. Near the field is a museum, in which many interesting relics are shown. At the village of Waterloo, just off the field, is the house where Wellington wrote his dispatch announcing the victory. Here may be seen the pencil with which he wrote. The boot of the Marquis of Anglesea, who lost a leg in the fight, is also on exhibition here.

In Brussels, as well as in all the cities of Belgium, Holland, and Germany, the sidewalks are covered with tables and chairs, where come the inhabitants to eat, drink, and smoke. Indeed, one is led to think, from the number of people to be seen sitting about town in front of eating and drinking places, that all they do is to cater to the wants of their stomachs. Everybody drinks here, from the little child hardly able to walk, to the old man with one foot in the grave. Beer and light wines are the principal beverages, and the price of them is very cheap. Notwithstanding all the liquor that is drank, there is hardly any drunkenness or rowdyism to be seen upon the streets. Everything is quiet and orderly, and in a city the size of Brussels, to say the least, it is surprising that such a state of things should exist. Very few arrests are made during the week. Sunday is a galaday, and the stores are all open, the saloons are in full blast, numerous concerts, theatres, etc., may be attended, and there is nothing to remind one that it is the sabbath.

From Brussels we went to the city of perfume, Cologne, of which I will speak in my next letter.

V.

WE arrived in Cologne on an afternoon of a very hot day, the 22d of July, tired and dusty, and the first thing that several of the male members of the party did was to take a bath in the river Rhine, in one of those splendid bath-houses so common in Europe. We came out of it greatly refreshed, and in spirits sufficiently exuberant to permit us to indulge in considerable sight-seeing before we retired that night.

Cologne is the oldest town on the Rhine. It is built in the shape of a crescent, and is inclosed with seven miles of wall, besides numerous ramparts and deep ditches. It is very irregularly built, and many of the streets are narrow and ill-paved. Cologne reminds me of Philadelphia, inasmuch as its sewage flows along the sides of the streets, but it is not nearly as clean a place as the "City of Quakers." I don't wonder that Coleridge wrote : —

> " The river Rhine, it is well known,
> Doth wash the city of Cologne :
> But tell me, nymphs, what power divine
> Shall henceforth wash the river Rhine?"

The sidewalks are horrible; in fact, there are no sidewalks of any account, and people as well as horses wend their way in the middle of the street.

The principal things for which the city is noted are its cathedral and cologne water. The former is one of the wonders of the world, and is a magnificent specimen of Gothic architecture. It was commenced in 1248, and proceeded slowly until the sixteenth century, when it was left in an incomplete state. Not until 1816 were any steps taken to save it from falling into decay;

in that year King Frederick William III. caused an enormous amount of money to be spent upon it. William IV. continued the restoration, and the best Gothic architects of the day were set to work upon it; but the plans of the cathedral are so extensive and elaborate that it is not yet completed, nor will it be for a number of years. Two hundred thousand dollars are annually appropriated for the building of the edifice. It stands upon a portion of the old Roman camp-ground. Countless sums of money have been expended on it in its day, and numerous have been the bequests made to it. Some idea of the vastness of the cathedral may be had from the figures representing its dimensions. The interior is four hundred and thirty feet long, and one hundred and forty feet broad; the transept, two hundred and thirty-four feet long ; and the choir, one hundred and forty feet high. The part which is appropriated for divine services occupies an area of seventy thousand square feet. When completed it will be five hundred and twenty-five feet high. The interior of the cathedral is wonderfully grand, and demands careful inspection. It is rich in details. There are seven chapels, containing many rare pictures, decorated altars, and relics. The most celebrated is that known as the Chapel of the Three Magi, in which is a gorgeous casket protected by a cover richly ornamented and set with precious stones. Beneath this are the tops of three skulls bearing golden crowns. These are said to have rested upon the shoulders of the wise men of the East who figured at the adoration of our Saviour. After being told this piece of information by the guide, with much mystery and solemnity, one feels like putting to him the interrogation which our American humorist, Mark Twain, in his "Innocents Abroad," says he so often used, — "Is he dead?" The treasury of the cathedral is exceedingly rich, and contains costly gold and silver church vessels, magnificent vestments for priests, etc. Among the things to be seen is a sort of frame-work in which the consecrated wafer is held up to view before the congregation in Roman Catholic churches. It is over a foot and a half high, of solid gold, and weighs over ten pounds. It is studded with large jewels, and must have cost a fortune. The stained-glass windows in the church are splendid specimens of workmanship. There are a number of tombs in the church, which contain the remains of eminent men. From the steeple, a beautiful view may be had of the Rhine and the lovely surrounding landscape. You can see the river winding on its course far in the distance, and look upon the vine-clad hills green as emerald for miles and miles.

Associated with Cologne, of course, is its perfumery. One never thinks of the former without sniffing the scent of the latter, and it is the general impression that cologne-water is its chief article of commerce. Be that as it may, about every other store in the city has it exposed for sale, and all claim to have the "Original Jean Antoine Marie Farina." Most of it is very poor stuff, but the best cologne that is made can be bought at stores kept by descendants of old Farina himself, the location of which can be easily ascertained.

The church of St. Ursula, built in the eleventh century, is always visited by strangers, as it contains, it is said, the bones of eleven thousand virgins murdered in the city on their return from a pilgrimage to Rome. All the interior of the church is decorated with bones.

Cologne also boasts of a large museum and zoölogical gardens. A stroll along its wharves is interesting, especially in the morning, when they are all alive with traders.

The evening we passed here Gilmore's famous band gave a concert, which a number of our party attended. As of course the readers of the "Mirror" are aware, this organization is winning high encomiums in this country for its artistic rendering of the most difficult music. It created quite a *furore* in Paris at the Exposition.

What there is of interest in Cologne can soon be seen, and most travelers take their leave of it as did we, in a steamboat headed up the Rhine. Leaving the city, good views are obtained of the bridges, the cathedral, and the principal public buildings. The ride up the river is perfectly charming; the scenery is beautifully picturesque and interesting; the little villages on the banks, the vine-clad hills, little Gothic churches, large and stately castles, old romantic ruins, every one of which has a history, — all contribute to fill out a lovely picture. One of the objects which first attract the attention of an American in going up the Rhine, is the vineyards. The banks on both sides of the river, rising to the height of hundreds of feet, are covered with grape-vines arranged in terraces one above another. No wonder that the best and cheapest wines in the world are to be found in this region. And, speaking of wine, I will say right here, that in Germany and Switzerland wine can be bought for a mere song. That which at home costs three dollars a bottle, can be bought here for about one-third of that price. It flows almost as free as water, and everybody drinks it, from the high-est to the lowest, the oldest to the youngest. Occasionally we came to a bridge of boats, a section of which had to be detached to permit the steamer to pass. We were on the river all day and enjoyed ourselves hugely. Our destination was Bie-berich, but before we get off the boat I will say a word of " Bingen on the Rhine." We made a short stop at this town, so beautifully written about in the poem so familiar to us all, and a number of the passengers alighted from the steamer for the sake of being able to say that they had stepped foot in Bingen. It is a small place, very prettily situated, but not in itself particularly interesting. If it had not been for the poem I have referred to, it would never have been widely known. Large quantities of wine are made here, and the neighborhood abounds in lovely scenery. Much might be written about the points of interest which lie nestled among the hills between Cologne and Bieberich, but I will not trespass upon your space. It was nine o'clock in the evening when the steamer landed us at the last-named town, from which we were conveyed in carriages to Wiesbaden, a drive of several miles along a per-fectly level road arched with horse-chestnut trees. The road from the wharf to the hotel is as straight as engineering skill can make it, and it would make the owners of good horseflesh in New Hampshire wild with delight to have such a trotting-course in the immediate vicinity of their stables. Of Wiesba-den, the Newport of Europe, I will speak next time.

VI.

PARIS, FRANCE, August 9, 1878.

WIESBADEN, called the Newport of Europe, is one of the oldest watering-places in Germany, and was formerly almost as great a town for gambling as Baden-Baden. The chief attraction here is the Cursaal, where the gambling used to be carried on so extensively, the rooms being thronged with players and spectators from eleven A. M. to eleven P. M., the principal games played being roulette and *rouge-et-noir*. The Cursaal is furnished most elegantly, and surrounding it are a large park and pleasure-ground beautifully laid out with walks, arbors, ponds, fountains, etc. A band plays here frequently, and the scene in the evening, when the season is at its height, is gay in the extreme. It is a very fashionable watering-place, and large numbers of summer boarders come here every year. Its hotels, of which there are many, are exceedingly fine, and the drives about the place are charming. In one part of the town is located a mineral spring, from which boiling water flows. This water, it is claimed, possesses many medicinal properties, and hundreds of persons drink and bathe in it daily. The spring is covered by a small building, and the water is dealt out free by pretty German girls, who earn many a penny by their attractiveness and courtesy. Of course we all tasted the water; everybody does who goes there and can wait for it to cool, for as it comes from the spring it is so hot that a cast-iron throat would be required for its passage. There is nothing at all disagreeable about it, except the heat. In taste it is slightly saline.

Leaving Wiesbaden and its warm decoction of salt and water, we sped on to Frankfort-on-the-Main, remaining a sufficiently long time to see all the sights which this celebrated commercial city offers. Frankfort is pleasantly situated in the midst of a plain, and has many broad streets lined with large and fine residences. In one portion of the city, however, in that called the Jewish quarter, some streets are so narrow that two vehicles can not pass each other. Here the most squalid poverty prevails, and the buildings are very old and dilapidated, many of them being in the last stages of decay. Several years ago quite a number of buildings in the Jewish district were torn down, which had a beneficial effect in giving to the section a cleaner appearance. Here, in stores black with age, every description of cheap and second-hand merchandise is exposed for sale. Here we were shown the house in which the Rothschilds were born. At one time all the Jews in Frankfort were compelled to reside in this district, being kept in by gates at each end. Many of the Jews of to-day live in the most stately edifices of which the city can boast.

Here in Frankfort is the house in which Goethe was born, and in a public square is a handsome monument of Gutenberg, Faust, and Schœffer. Drainage is carried on here according to the most improved plan, at an enormous expense. The town is surrounded with public grounds tastefully laid out. The cathedral here is remarkable rather for its historical associations than for any intrinsic beauty or elegance; indeed, it is very plain inside. It was founded in 1238. Its height is two hundred and sixty feet. Forty-six German emperors have been crowned in the cathedral. Near the cathedral is an old house at which Martin Luther stopped on his way to Worms. Frankfort has an old bridge, built in 1342, which seems as firm and substantial as though it was constructed only yesterday. The center is adorned with a statue of Charlemagne, near which is a cock, the latter being, it is said, erected to commemorate the story, that, whereas, by private compact between the devil and the architect, the first living thing that crossed was to be sacrificed to the former, it was arranged for a cock to be the victim.

After leaving Frankfort, Heidelberg was the place at which we took up our abode, and a glorious old town it is, rich in his-

.torical associations, as all readers are aware. Few towns are more charmingly situated or possess a more picturesque appearance. Five times the town has been bombarded, twice reduced to ashes, and three times its inhabitants were given over to the rapine and plunder of soldiery. Having suffered so much from the ravages of war, Heidelberg is now comparatively a modern town. The attraction which has the most fascination for the tourist is the old castle, a most imposing and magnificent ruin, with lofty turrets, great, round towers, terraces, archways, and court-yards. It is called the most splendid ruin in all Europe. It is a wonderful mingling of fortress and palace. Its foundation dates back to the thirteenth century, and fortunes were spent in its construction. No modern structure I have ever seen compares for a moment with this castle in solidity and architectural grandeur. As you look upon it in all its vastness, you can hardly believe that human agency created it. Here are walls twenty-five feet thick, and the rest of the castle is built on the same gigantic plan. I cannot, of course, describe in the limits of a letter the vast extent and splendor of this castle. One might stay here for days and make new discoveries almost hourly. The castle is covered with figures of the most beautiful design, chiseled out of the solid stone.

The eye is bewildered with the profusion of the works of art, which are the result of six centuries of labor. The castle is situated upon a high hill, only accessible from two points. The view from many spots about the grounds is very extensive and pleasing. Before leaving the castle I must speak of the wine-cellar. Here may be seen barrels as large as cottage houses, in which the lordly occupants of the castle kept their wine. One of these hogsheads when filled holds two hundred and thirty-six thousand bottles. On the top of it, which is reached by a flight of stairs, is laid a platform, upon which many a quadrille has been danced.

The University of Heidelberg is justly and widely celebrated as a school of law and medicine, and from its walls many illustrious scholars have gone forth. The buildings are very plain and unpretentious looking. About eight hundred students at present are in attendance at the university. It was founded in 1386. The library of the institution is a very valuable one. In 1662, after bombarding the town, Tilly is said to have used a part of the contents of this library as litter for his horses. The students are stalwart-looking fellows, who appear to take life easy. They may be seen about town at most any hour of the day, and nearly every one you meet has his face disfigured with scars, the result of duels, which are of very common occurrence among those who pursue their studies at the university. Some of the faces I saw were horribly scarred, bearing great gashes six inches long. All disputes of a serious nature are settled by a duel, and a student who refuses to fight is ever after looked upon with contempt. Indeed, so thoroughly has this idea of dueling been engrafted into the German mind, that I doubt if one of the eight hundred students in the institution would decline a challenge to meet an opponent. Moreover, it is considered a mark of glory and honor to be the possessor of one or more scars. The dueling-grounds of the students are situated near the buildings, but strangers are not allowed to witness any of the contests. The style of dueling here is peculiar. The students are well swathed in wadding, linen, and cord, and the face is the point at which thrusts are made. Occasionally a duel terminates fatally. The faculty evidently look with favor upon this mode of settling disputes, as they take no steps to put a stop to it. The students wear different colored caps, to designate the corps to which they belong.

Beautiful meerschaum pipes can be bought in Heidelberg, at very low prices; also, many curiously carved articles of ivory.

In connection with the students, I forgot to mention that there are certain clubs famed for the number of glasses of beer which the members can drink. No one can join them until he disposes of the prescribed amount of beer; and the president of the club is he who can hold the largest number of glasses. The beer-gardens here, as the reader will doubtless imagine, are very liberally patronized by the students.

The surroundings of Heidelberg are very romantic, and many delightful excursions can be made to the adjacent districts.

VII.

AFTER leaving Heidelberg we went to Baden-Baden, the gayest of the gay watering-places in Europe, although its glory and brightness have somewhat paled since the gambling-houses have been shut up. In the height of the summer season, and we were fortunately there at that time, the town is crowded with visitors; and of an evening or late in the afternoon, the scene upon the principal streets, alive with handsome equipages and richly dressed promenaders, is ever changing and gay in the extreme. The aristocracy and wealth of numerous nations may be seen here. Baden lies at the entrance of the celebrated Black Forest, which, tradition tells us, was inhabited by giants, dwarfs, and all sorts of spirits. The drives about the place are delightful, and along the bank of the River Ouse is a splendid, broad, level road, which is at certain hours thronged with vehicles. The hotels here are large, comfortable, and well-kept, and the prices charged are in great contrast with the exorbitant demands of Saratoga and Newport and other first-class summer resorts in America. In the center of nearly all the hotels on the continent is a large court-yard, without a roof, and provided with tables and chairs, and adorned and made beautiful and attractive with flowers, fountains, luxuriant potted plants, etc. Here you can sit in the shade with pleasant surroundings, and enjoy yourself in a quiet and comfortable manner.

One of the attractions here which strangers always visit, is the great gaming-house, where thousands of francs have been lost and won in a single night. It is an enormous building, beautifully fitted up with drawing-rooms, elegant ball-rooms, reading-room, band-room, etc. The most artistic paintings adorn the walls, and the chandeliers are gorgeous. The furniture in these rooms is of the richest kind, and all the appointments are of a palatial order. Magnificent gardens, which have been made strikingly beautiful by means of a profusion of flowers, plants, trees, statues, etc., surround the building, and here in the evening crowds of people gather to listen to charming music by a band, eat ice-cream, drink wine, chat, walk, and have a good time. A small admission fee is charged to enter the building, which is used now for balls, etc. Standing in the main room, in which the tiger a few years since was so extensively fought, your fancy hears the rattle of the roulette wheel, the chink of gold and silver, and the clatter of tongues. Around the tables here people of every condition and profession in life assembled, ladies as well as gentlemen, professional gamblers and inexperienced youths, counts and adventuresome Americans, — all worshiping at the same gilded altar, over which the pall has long since fallen. Like Wiesbaden, this place also has a mineral spring, the waters of which are each year quaffed by thousands. The empress paid the town a flying visit while we were there, and a number of festivities were inaugurated in her honor, and hundreds of banners were thrown to the breeze. I got a glimpse of the carriage in which she was taking a drive, but failed to see her. The equipage was a very imposing affair.

A two hours' ride from Baden-Baden is the old city of Strasbourg, celebrated for its magnificent cathedral and wonderful clock. The cathedral is the highest in the world, towering four hundred and sixty-eight feet, and is rich in beautiful and artistic carvings and statues. We forbear giving a detailed description of it. Its length is six hundred and twenty-five feet, and breadth one hundred and ninety-five feet. Its great stained-glass windows, representing scriptural subjects, are wondrously beautiful. The cathedral was commenced in 1015, and the original plans are preserved in the town. The great astronomical clock is located inside the cathedral, and, as every one knows, is a wonderful piece of mechanism. At twelve o'clock, figures representing the twelve apostles pass in procession before the Saviour, who blesses each, and a cock crows; the devil is seen looking out of a window, and a cupid turns an hour-glass, etc., etc. At the quarters, a little child, youth, manhood, and old age respectively appear. Then connected with the clock are a perpetual calendar and a celestial globe, and numerous other ingenious contrivances. The model of this clock which has been quite extensively exhibited in the United States, is a faithful representation of the original.

September 28, 1870, Strasbourg surrendered to the German army, and signs of the five weeks' bombardment which it experienced are visible in many places. The cathedral was slightly damaged during the engagement. At present, the town is constructing fortifications on a very extensive scale, and the next time, if ever, it is attacked, the besiegers will find it more of an undertaking to capture the place than did the army eight years ago. Strasbourg claims the honor of being the birth-place of printing, and a statue of Gutenberg adorns a place named after him.

The place is celebrated in the estimation of gourmands for the rich *pates*, known as *pates de foie gras*. These are made from the livers of geese, the said livers being of enormous size, made so by cruel treatment of the unfortunate birds. The storks of Strasbourg are more fortunate, being received and treated by the inhabitants with the greatest hospitality. As a result, the town is alive with them. They build their nests, huge affairs, on the chimney-tops. So much do the people think of these ungainly looking birds, that they consider it as a sure presage of coming good fortune to the inhabitants of the dwelling which a stork selects for his home. The same super-stition prevails also in Holland.

A spot on the Rhine where every tourist should spend a day, is at Neuhausen, where the falls of the Rhine are located. The place is one of great interest from the beauty of the river at this point. The Rhine above the falls is about three hundred feet wide, and the height of the falls is about sixty feet on one side and forty-five on the other; the water rushes in three leaps with a volume of about one hundred thousand cubic feet per second, and then falls into a large basin. The spectacle is one of true beauty and grandeur, although it does not approximate the magnificence of Niagara.

I crossed the river just below the falls in a boat rowed by two brawny-armed specimens of mountaineers, and enjoyed the novel experience of being on water which boiled and bubbled with a deafening roar, being lashed to foam by the tremendous volume of water which came tumbling down over the rocks. On a high eminence overlooking the falls, is an old castle from which a fine view of the river is obtainable. At several places on the grounds projections are built out into the river, where the full power, force, and grandeur of the falls may be appreciated. Here rubber coats are put on, as the spray dashes about continually. At the castle will be found a good collection of Swiss carvings, photographs, curiosities, etc. The color of the river at Neuhausen is in striking contrast to what it is from Cologne to Bieberich, being all the way between those places dirty and muddy in appearance, while here it is clear and very green.

Zurich was our next stopping-place, which was reached after a delightful ride of a few hours through a country abounding in beautiful scenery. We were particularly struck with the little country stations which we were whirled rapidly past. They are very pretty rustic Swiss cottages, covered with running vines, and the yards about them are radiant in blossoms of many hues. Everything about these stations is kept in perfect order, and the places are exceedingly inviting. At every railroad crossing we noticed a uniformed guard stationed, with a musket at his shoulder, to prevent the possibility of an accident by persons going over the track near the time when a train is due. The railroad system here is much superior to ours in America, every precaution to guard against accidents being taken, and it is very seldom that any traveler is injured. An American can make journeys on the cars here with much greater comfort than he can at home. You can always tell when a train is to start by a whistle from the engine, there being no unnecessary ringing of bells. Numerous guards accompany each train, and they will answer any number of questions for you in the most civil manner, and render any necessary assistance about luggage. There is no confusion and hubbub at the stations; everything moves on smoothly, and you are not in any danger of being run over by a truck loaded with trunks.

The road-beds are better than a majority of those in America, being to a great extent macadamized, and consequently the trains run very smoothly. One thing about English locomotives that particularly pleases an American is the absence of cinders and dirt while riding in the cars. You can keep your head out of the window for an hour at a time and the chances are that you will not get a speck of dirt in your eyes, the cinders being nearly all consumed. But, notwithstanding these advantages which I have mentioned, we can still teach them something about railroading.

Leaving the subject of railroads, we will return to Zurich long enough to say a single word about this lovely town. Zurich is situated on the shores of a beautiful lake about twenty-five miles in length, around several sides of which high mountains tower heavenward, forming an appropriate frame for the pleasing picture nestling in the valley. One of these mountains, covered with snow, lifts its peak ten thousand feet. The hotel at which we stopped, *Belle Vue,* is situated on the edge of the lake, and from the windows of one side a stone can be tossed into the waters below, It was here that General Grant stopped a few weeks since. We were shown the apartments which he occupied. They were very elegantly fitted up, rich crimson velvet forming the covering of the furniture. The attractions in Zurich are not many, but it is a splendid place to spend a few days, and is quite extensively patronized by travelers. The lake is the abode of numerous varieties of the finny tribe, and its waters are fished considerably. We went from Zurich to Lucerne.

VIII.

Paris, France, August 19, 1878.

I T was at the lovely town of Lucerne that we headquartered next after leaving Zurich, and we remained in that vicinity several days. It is a very fashionable resort, no one thinking of making a tour of Europe without going there. In consequence of the large tide of tourists which sweeps in upon Lucerne each summer, a number of magnificent hotels have been erected, one of which, the Schweizerhof, is regarded as the finest hotel on the continent. Lucerne is most beautifully situated on the shores of that sheet of water bearing the same name as the town, of whose loveliness poets have so often sung. And the subject well merits all that has been said in its favor; for it is indeed a charming lake, most romantically located at the foot of mountains which tower thousands of feet into the air. The lake, besides being called Lucerne, is known as the Lake of the Four Cantons. It is considered the most beautiful body of water in all Switzerland, and the grandeur and beauty of the scenery on every side are heightened by the historical associations connected with the country bordering on its waters; for these cantons are the birthplace of Switzerland's freedom, and the scenes of the struggles of William Tell and his brave associates.

A few miles' ride on the lake brings you to Tell's chapel, situated upon a rock on the shore, and marking the place where Tell sprang out of Gessler's boat, as is told in the stories of the Swiss hero. One of the principal sights in Lucerne is a lion sculptured out of the solid rock by the celebrated Danish sculptor, Thorwaldsen, in memory of the Swiss guard that were massacred in defense of the Tuileries in 1792. The figure is in a beautiful grotto, a sheet of water, and, as a work of art, is truly magnificent, being most admirable in conception and execution. This colossal piece of sculpture, twenty-eight and one-half feet long and eighteen feet high, represents a dying lion with his side transfixed by a broken spear, protecting the shield of the Bourbons, even in the agonies of death. Near the lion is a chapel, where on the tenth of August a special solemn mass is celebrated in memory of the slain. In the immediate neighborhood of the lion is the celebrated Glacier Garden, where are to be seen most wonderful geological phenomena in the shape of what are called "Giant Pots," or huge excavations in the solid rock. Some of these are thirty feet deep and seventy-five feet in circumference, and at the bottom may be seen the bowlders which brought these "pots" into existence. Glacial action was undoubtedly the agent which was chiefly instrumental in producing these results, but the glaciers were of much greater magnitude than any which now exist. The rocks in this locality are very much grooved, revealing clearly that huge rivers of snow and ice passed down the mountain side.

The walls and watch-towers of Lucerne date back to the fourteenth century, when the town occupied a far more prominent position among the Swiss towns than at present. Its population is about sixteen thousand. Lucerne has two very old and interesting bridges, one of which dates back to the beginning of the fourteenth century. It is decorated with one hundred and fifty-four curious paintings, so suspended that any one crossing from the north side beholds in succession seventy-seven scenes from the lives of the joint patron saints of the town, but coming in the opposite direction the scenes are commemorative of events in the history of the Swiss Confederation. In the other bridge the Dance of Death is quaintly depicted. The arsenal of Lucerne abounds in objects of interest. The reputed sword of Tell is shown here, also axes and suits of armor from old battlefields.

One of the greatest attractions is the old cathedral, where every evening may be heard one of the finest organs in the world. We enjoyed an hour's concert, which was marvelously fine. The organ possesses wonderful power, and its tone is peculiarly sweet and clear. The man who presided at the instrument is an old and talented performer, and his efforts are masterpieces. The selections rendered embraced a variety of styles, adapted to display to the best advantage the possibilities of the organ. The piece, however, which represented a thunder-storm among the Alps, elicited from our party, as it always does from everybody, the most praise. It was indeed a marvelous performance, intensely realistic. The rattle and trickle of rain-drops, the fitful gusts of the rising tempest, and the muttering of the distant thunder were first heard. Gradually the tempest increased, the thunder roared, the rain fell in torrents, the wind howled and shrieked, and the swollen streams came rushing down the mountain. Then the peals gradually subsided and rolled slowly off among the mountains, the wind abated, and the rain ceased; and the notes of a small organ, as if in a convent or chapel near by, were heard, and then arose a chant so sweet and clear that it seemed as if the voices of the world's choicest singers were assembled together. This chant by invisible voices finally burst into a glorious hymn of praise, and then gradually faded away as though one by one the singers were quietly departing. The effect of the thunder-storm and its peaceful termination was singularly grand and sweet, and the audience listened spell-bound. It seemed too real to be the result of the fingers of an organist upon his instrument. The performance is one that, once heard, never will be forgotten. The *vox-humana* stop of the organ surpasses any thing of the kind in the world. It is this which causes the sweet sounds so surprisingly life-like and clear.

At Lucerne, very beautiful articles of Swiss handiwork may be bought very cheap. Besides carvings and ingenious works of art, the most exquisitely embroidered handkerchiefs are for sale here at very reasonable prices. Some of these handkerchiefs are wonderful specimens of skill with the needle, the most beautiful and intricate patterns being worked upon them. The Swiss girls who do this kind of work can pursue it only a few hours each day, as it is exceedingly tedious and causes a great strain upon the eyes. While at Lucerne our party made an excursion to the Righi, one of the most famous of the mountains of Switzerland.

The Righi consists of a series of peaks, the highest of which falls a little below Mt. Washington. There is a railway up the mountain, patterned after our famous one in New Hampshire. Its length is three and one-half miles, and the labor of constructing it required the expenditure of a vast amount of money. The views which we enjoyed in ascending were beautiful in the extreme; but, fine as they were, they but faintly foreshadowed what we were to see that evening when the sun should set. When the summit was nearly reached a cloud covered the lowlands and shut out our view, and we feared that we should be unable to see Righi in all its loveliness. Towards evening, however, the clouds rolled away and the sun burst forth in all its splendor, revealing a spectacle most grand and magnificent. Lake Lucerne was at our feet; and eight other Swiss lakes, calm and still, and looking like plates of polished steel, rested on the landscape and flashed in the sunbeams. Silver ribbons of rivers glittered on the bosom of the earth like necklaces, and the innumerable little Swiss villages, scattered about on the rich dark green carpet of verdure, made a picture that defies description. All around, their summits covered with snow, rise mountains ten and twelve thousand feet into the air, the effect of the sun's rays upon which is strikingly splendid. They seemed to be all afire. Gradually the shadows deepen. The sun is sinking. The blaze is becoming fainter, and we perceive the sun go down, — a huge ball of fire. Its light is extinguished and night is fast settling around. We turn and go to the hotel and exhaust our vocabulary of terms of admiration over the grand spectacle we have just witnessed. We retired early that night, and at three o'clock were aroused by the Alpine horn breaking sweet and clear upon the still mountain air. We dressed ourselves hurriedly and went out of doors, eager to catch the first glimpse of the sunrise which we were assured would be infinitely superior to the sunset, and, to be brief, indeed it was, surpassing anything of the kind any of us had ever witnessed. After enjoying the glorious scene until the sun was well up in the heavens, with our appetites well sharpened we repaired to the hotel for breakfast, and subsequently descended the mountain. There was little to be seen going down on account of a dense fog which enveloped us, and, on arriving at the base, the spot which an hour before we had left radiant in sunshine, we beheld now all dark and gloomy. The changes on the Righi are very abrupt.

Bidding adieu to Lucerne, we proceeded by steamer across the lake to Alpnach, and then by stage to Brienz through the famous Brunig Pass. At Brienz we proceeded by steamer over Lake Thun to Giessbach.

The journey occupied nearly an entire day and was romantically interesting and pleasing, fine and varied views abounding. The Brunig road is a wonderful specimen of engineering skill, hardly a loose pebble being visible. The road winds round and round amid the most beautiful mountain scenery. Although the ascent is steady, it is rendered easy by numerous curves. At the summit of the pass the magnificent Meiringen valley bursts upon the view. This is, as it were, a level, beautiful country between two great ranges of mountains, and you stánd upon one and look down upon it and across to the other. Numerous waterfalls are to be seen dashing and tumbling down the mountain sides. From the summit to the bottom it is so far that your head swims as you look over the edge of the precipice, even if you are possessed of strong nerves, and the houses in the valley look like mere specks. The ride through the pass was grand in the extreme. At Giessbach, where we passed the night, one of the finest hotels in all Europe is located, at a height of about one thousand feet from the waters of Lake Thun. The attractions here are the splendid scenery, and the magnificent waterfalls, which are in close proximity to the house. In the evening the falls were illuminated, producing a spectacle most magnificent and picturesque. The falls descend about fourteen hundred feet in a series of seven beautiful cascades, leaping and tumbling down amid the verdant foliage. Under the influence of the lights thrown upon the falls, the water seemed to be first a mass of molten silver, then a rich, red-like flame, and again the hue changed and it became a deep purple, and finally green. Such a sight cannot be adequately described; it must be seen to be appreciated.

From Giessbach we went to Interlachen, a famous resort for tourists in Switzerland, as a place from which interesting excursions may be made. It is beautifully and romantically situated, and its hotels are noticeably good. From this town a splendid view of the Jungfrau, one of the best known of the mountains of Switzerland, is obtainable. While at Interlachen our party visited a glacier and went into it several hundred feet. The temperature, as may be imagined, was decidedly frigid.

After leaving Interlachen we made short stops at Berne, Freiburg, and Geneva, before going to Paris; but I will only speak briefly of the attractions in these places. Berne is a city of bears. That animal is the heraldic emblem of the city, and that fact is evident before a person has been there a single hour. They may be seen on the city gates in granite, carved out of wood by the hundreds in shop-windows, and alive and hungry for sweetmeats in the city bear-pits. Berne is a good place to buy wood-carvings, cuckoo-clocks, and music-boxes. The town has a tower of very old origin, on which is a curious automatic clock, a peculiar feature of which is at every hour a troop of bears appear in front and march round a wooden platform; a cock also crows, and a comical figure strikes a bell with a hammer. Fortunately we were there on a market-day, when the streets were thronged with people, affording us a fine opportunity for studying the manners, customs, and acts of the Swiss peasantry. The streets were lined with booths and stalls, and the whole scene looked like a large country-fair. Berne boasts of a cathedral two hundred and thirteen feet high, in which is a splendid organ, which all who go to the town should be sure to hear.

Freiburg is a curious town, outwardly and inwardly. Go to the upper part of the town, and everybody and everything is German; but in the lower part, everybody and everything is French. It is very hilly, and the streets are exceedingly steep.

There are three things which *must* be seen in Freiburg, and and many which may, if time permits. First, an old lime-tree, fourteen feet in circumference, its branches supported on stone pillars, — the cathedral and the suspension bridges. The lime-tree has quite a history, which in brief is this: When the memorable battle of Morat was being fought, the inhabitants of Freiburg assembled in the public square, waiting for tidings of the battle. One of the soldiers, knowing that his towns-people would be anxious to know how the battle went, started for the town as soon as the struggle was over, running at the top of his speed. On the way he met with an accident, falling down a steep embankment, by reason of a twig, which he grasped for support, coming out by the roots. He kept on, however, in spite of his wounds, and, still clutching the fatal twig, finally reached the market-place with only strength enough to shout: "Victory! Victory!" and fell dead in the midst of his friends. The twig was planted, and now the fine old lime-tree stands as a beautiful memento of the love and courage of that gallant young soldier, and the victory of Morat. This happened in 1481.

The cathedral is a Gothic building, dating from 1285, and is two hundred and eighty feet in height. The visitor will be struck with the remarkable bas-relief over the entrance, "The Last Judgment,"—an angel weighing mankind in batches, devils carting off the condemned, etc., etc. The organ here is one of the finest in the world. There are two performances on it daily, and a pleasant hour may be spent here listening to its strange and marvelous music. Some wonderful wind and storm effects are introduced by the organist. The organ has seventy-seven stops, and seven thousand eight hundred pipes, some of which are thirty-five feet high.

The suspension bridge thrown across the river Sarne is the longest in Europe, and is a wonderfully artistic piece of workmanship. It has a span of nine hundred and sixty-four feet, and its cost was about one hundred and twenty-five thousand dollars. It is light and elegant, and yet amazingly strong. Across the Gotteron ravine is another bridge seven hundred and forty-six feet long, and three hundred and five feet above the water. It is fastened into the solid rock, and looks, from its slight and delicate make, like a mere chain thrown from one side of the gorge to the other.

From Freiburg we sped on to Geneva, crossing Lake Leman,

the largest sheet of water in Switzerland, and with which everybody who has read Byron is familiar. Its waters are as blue as indigo, and the scenery around its shores is charmingly beautiful. Geneva is the most thickly populated town in Switzerland; it is divided by the River Rhone into two parts, and this natural division has almost as naturally separated the inhabitants into two classes. The chief manufacture of the town is watches, of which about one hundred thousand are turned out annually. In the production of these, an amazing quantity of gold, silver, and precious stones is made use of.

The visitor will find a splendid assortment of jewelry in some of the stores of Geneva. Imitation jewelry is not allowed to be sold here, unless so labeled. The sights here are not many and are easily seen. They are a large and fine museum, a cathedral, the house where Rousseau was born, the house where Calvin lived for nineteen years and died, an arsenal in which are preserved many specimens of Swiss arms, the Church of the Madeline, built in the tenth century, the City Hall, where the business of the Geneva arbitration was transacted, and the watch and music-box manufactories. Before closing I will say a word about music-boxes. I visited one of the largest manufactories here, and was greatly surprised to learn in what a variety of styles music-boxes are made. They were for sale here at prices from a few francs to three thousand dollars, and in all the forms that the minds of cunning artisans can devise. There were chairs which would play when you sat in them; albums which went off into a waltz if you opened them; pitchers, vases, and dishes which would strike up a tune when you lifted them from the table; hat-racks which would produce sweet sounds as soon as a *chapeau* was placed upon them, etc., etc. The music-box factory was one of the most interesting places we visited in Geneva, and we were greatly amused at what we saw and heard there. From Geneva we obtained a fine view of Mt. Blanc, with its snowy summit rising high into the heavens. From Geneva we went direct to Paris, of which I will speak in my next letter.

IX.

THE sights and scenes of Paris have been so often and so thoroughly described in every style and vein, that it seems as though everybody ought to be perfectly familiar with this, the gayest of gay cities, and that everything that possibly could be said in regard to it has been penned; but, as I have given short descriptions of the other places visited by our party, I will not omit this fashionable and fascinating metropolis from the list, and as briefly as possible will speak of its principal points of interest, and a few of the many impressions which Parisian life made upon me. Of course, the great center of attraction now is the Grand Exposition; but, as recollections of our own Centennial are still fresh in our minds, we will leave that to be dealt with finally. There is so much to see and do that weeks could be most profitably spent here; and, although during the eight days of my stay I was constantly upon the move and visited the lions of the city, I feel as though I had but made a beginning, and a small one at that, towards "doing" it. We reached Paris about six o'clock on the morning of August 10, after a fifteen hours' ride in the cars from Geneva, and our first impressions of it as we rode in carriages to the hotel were received while we were in a very jaded and worn-out state, the result of our long and wearisome journey. However, notwithstanding the fact that we greatly needed rest, we all started out sight-seeing immediately after breakfast. Without any regard to the order in which we visited the famous places, I will briefly allude to them.

The Arch of Triumph, a magnificent piece of architecture, erected by the first Napoleon at a cost of over two million dollars, is at the head of the *Avenue des Champs Elysees*, and is visible from almost any point in the city, being one of the landmarks by which strangers keep their bearings while wandering about Paris. The arch is one hundred and fifty feet high, and one hundred and thirty-seven feet wide, and is covered with groups of carved figures representing warlike scenes, etc. Inside the arch the names of many French generals are carved, also the names of numerous famous battles. This splendid monument to Napoleon was completed in 1836, after thirty years of labor upon it. From the summit of the arch a fine view of the city may be had. Many persons ascend the arch on their first visit to Paris as soon as they arrive, in order to obtain an idea of the size and shape of the city. Fifteen persons have thrown themselves from the top of the arch and were dashed to pieces on the pavement below. A surer means of death could not be sought.

The Louvre is a name associated with which are priceless artistic treasures. It is generally known that here may be seen the rarest and most magnificent works of art of which the world can boast, and to attempt in a few words to give an idea of its extent and greatness seems almost futile. In size the Louvre is perfectly colossal, and it covers acres of ground. Millions of dollars have been spent upon the buildings. All along the front are statues of distinguished men of France, and numerous architectural devices adorn various portions of the exterior, and the work of improvement is still going on. Inside of the Louvre the lover of art can revel in wonderful specimens. Days may be employed here with profit. The number of pictures and statues here staggers one on account of their vastness. Why, a catalogue of the contents of the Louvre makes a book of nearly a thousand pages! The Louvre is a great exposition in itself, and the position which it occupies in the estimation of the world is evident from the thousands of people who visit it yearly. Here may be seen almost endless halls filled with sculpture, statuary, and paintings, known all over the world by copies and engravings. One takes infinite delight in looking upon the great originals, collected with so much care and at such an enormous expense. We look upon a perfect host of masterpieces. Here are pictures by Titian, Rubens, Vandyke, Leonardo da Vinci, Murillo, Raphael, Guido, Rembrandt, Claude Lorraine, and others of the world's celebrated artists. You can look upon Murillo's "Conception of the Virgin," which cost twenty-four thousand six hundred pounds ; Titian's "Entombment of Christ," and a host of other famous paintings. Before the great masterpieces there may almost always be seen artists making copies, which reminds me that in one of the German árt galleries I saw a man without arms, who was copying, with wonderful accuracy, a famous painting, holding the brush between the toes of the right foot. It was astonishing to behold the fine work which was being executed in this strange manner, and served as a striking illustration of the possibilities which lie in members of the human body. There is in the Louvre a room devoted to the relics of the first Napoleon, which is always visited with much interest. Among other things is a lock of the emperor's hair, his sword, whip, and saddle, the handkerchief used by him on his death-bed, clothes which he wore when he landed at Elba, etc. Fresh surprises are constantly greeting the visitor to the Louvre, and a day spent in it can hardly fail to create enthusiasm in the most indifferent to the beauties of art.

The Tomb of Bonaparte is a most magnificent affair, located in the Church of the Invalides. An altar, crypt, and sarcophagus constitute the tomb. The altar is very large and beautiful, being constructed of large columns of marble supporting a canopy of white and gold, beneath which is the figure of the Saviour on the cross. Through large windows of colored glass come rays of light, which, falling upon the altar, transform it into a blaze of glory. The effect is truly beautiful.

In the center of the church beneath the dome is the crypt, a great circular opening thirty-six feet in diameter by twenty feet deep. A marble rail surrounds it. Below is the sarcophagus, wherein lies all that remains of the great French emperor. The sarcophagus is a huge and elegant structure of red granite or porphyry. Its weight is one hundred and thirty-five thousand pounds, and it was brought from Finland at a cost of thirty thousand dollars. The pavement of the crypt is of exquisite mosaic work in marble. Around the sarcophagus stand twelve colossal figures representing victories. In a chapel adjoining is the sword of Austerlitz, and groups of flags captured by the French, and other mementoes. The tomb with all its details cost nearly two millions of dollars. In chapels about the church are other splendid monuments to distinguished persons, among which is the tomb of Napoleon's eldest brother, Joseph, king of Spain. The whole interior of the Church of the Invalides is upon an elaborate scale. The frescoing upon the walls is strikingly rich and artistic.

Pere la Chaise, one of the largest burial-grounds in the world, contains over twenty thousand tombs, thousands of graves, and occupies two hundred and twelve acres of ground. Some parts of it present a dilapidated appearance; but, as a whole, it is laid out in a very pleasing manner, with walks and drives. Without a guide, traveling here is not advisable, as one is certain to get lost in this city of the dead. In Pere la Chaise may be seen monuments and slabs of every conceivable design, costing from a few cents up to thousands of dollars. These tombs, many of them, are very curious affairs, and some are really comical in appearance, looking like a half-finished hut of marble. Within the tombs are mementoes of every description, and in most of them are gay altars. I noticed in several where little children were buried, dolls and various kinds of toys. We visited the Jewish portion of the cemetery first. This is separated from the rest by a wall. Here we saw the monument of Rachel, the celebrated actress; also one on which was inscribed the name of Rothschild. As one walks about the cemetery he constantly sees well-known names, distinguished in art, science, literature, and arms. Here is Beranger, the poet; Laplace, the astronomer; Racine, the poet; Scribe, the dramatist; Talma, the actor. Here, in a lot encircled with a plain iron fence covered with ivy, sleeps Marshal Ney, a hero of a hundred battles, Napoleon's bravest officer. We saw the monument in which Thiers, the great French statesman, was but a short time since placed. It was literally covered with mementoes, and hundreds of names were written upon the walls in pencil. It was very interesting to wander about here, and look upon the spots where distinguished men are buried, but we must not linger longer.

The grand old cathedral of Notre Dame has for centuries held a prominent place in the history of Paris, and its general appearance is familiar to the world. In structure it is Gothic, and its two towers are over two hundred feet in height. It is rich in ornamentation and carving, and the interior is grand and impressive. It has suffered a great deal, as is evident, from the rough hands of revolutionists. The stained-glass windows in it, of enormous size, are magnificent. It is situated close to the River Seine, and from its towers a fine view of the city may be had. Near Notre Dame is the Morgue, which a number of our party visited. It is constructed on the same principle of morgues generally, and is not particularly worthy of comment.

The Church of the Madeleine is one of the first public buildings the tourist recognizes in Paris. This structure is magnificent and imposing, with its fifty-two Corinthian columns, its noble front, bronze entrance, and doors thirty feet high, reached by a long flight of marble steps. The interior is one spacious hall, the floors and walls of which are all solid marble, beautifully decorated, and lighted from the top by domes. All along the sides are chapels dedicated to different saints and adorned with elegant statues and paintings. The high altar is rich in beautiful sculpture, the principal group representing Mary Magdalene borne into paradise by angels. It is most exquisitely done. The edifice is situated in a broad, open square, near the central part of the city. The church cost two and one-half millions of dollars.

The Church of St. Genevieve, or the Pantheon, is another magnificent structure, three hundred and fifty feet long and two hundred and sixty feet wide, surrounded by Corinthian columns. The interior is beautiful in the extreme. In vaults in the church the remains of Mirabeau and Murat were deposited.

The Garden of Plants is one of the very enjoyable places in Paris, where the visitor can gratify his taste for zoölogy, botany, and natural science. In the large and beautiful garden are spacious hot-houses and greenhouses, containing every variety of rare plants, a botanical garden, galleries of botany, zoölogy, and mineralogy. The different museums are rich in rare specimens of their departments. The grounds are most beautifully laid out in handsome walks, with parterres of flowers, shade-trees, shrubs, etc.

At the Palace of the Luxembourg may be seen a superb collection of modern paintings, and a visit to this place should not be omitted by a lover of art.

One of the greatest attractions about Paris is Versailles, situated a few miles outside of the city. This palace and its surroundings stand as a memorial of the prodigality which characterized the reign of Louis XIV. Over two hundred million dollars have been expended upon this great permanent French exposition and historical museum of the French nation. One of the parks about the palace covers forty acres. I will not attempt a description of Versailles, for the subject is too vast to grasp in a limited space. Everything about the palace is characterized by magnificence and splendor, and the visitor here revels in beauty and elegance, the like of which he can see nowhere else. Wonders of art in painting, sculpture, and decoration may be seen in profusion, and one is dazzled at the lavish display, and his eyes ache and his limbs are weary before he has seen one-quarter of what this extraordinary palace offers. The grounds about the palace are in keeping with the splendor within, and it seems as though one was in fairy-land as he walks about the beautiful parks among flowers and fountains and fine groves. No one should go to Paris without visiting Versailles.

The display of goods in the various stores of Paris is something most remarkable, and it is a great treat to walk through some of the main thoroughfares and gaze into the windows at what is exposed there for sale. Everything, almost, that the ingenuity of the whole world can devise may be seen. But an American who unattended attempts to buy anything in these stores will not obtain the articles at prices at all approximating what a Frenchman would pay for them. The entrance of an American or an Englishman is a signal for increasing the regular price of every article which he desires to purchase, and, unless he is very careful, goods of an inferior quality will be palmed off upon him. Frenchmen have no consciences, and it never enters the heads of these smirking, supple-jointed swindlers that a reputation for honesty and fair dealing is worth anything at all to their establishments.

In some of the largest places of business all the goods are marked in plain figures so that a customer can see the price, from which there is no deviation. If an American desires to shop successfully and cheaply in Paris, he should get a French person to accompany him. With some branches of business the law is very stringent, and species of barefaced cheating, such as may every day be seen in New York, are prevented. Dealers in imitation jewelry dare not sell it for gold. They are compelled to label the articles "imitation." This has caused dealers to exhaust a great deal of skill in the production of splendid imitations, and for a few francs an article may be bought which has every appearance of having cost hundreds. There are many French articles which have a large sale in America, which it is hard to find in Paris. But, really, it seems as if everything ever heard of or thought of could be bought in the French capital, and made in any style, prepared in any form, and furnished with marvelous speed. There is one characteristic of the French shopman which contrasts agreeably with American dealers, and that is their willingness to make or alter an article to the purchaser's taste. If a lady likes the sleeves of one cloak and the body of another, she is informed that the change of sleeves shall instantly be made. Shopkeepers will put themselves to almost any inconvenience to cater to the tastes of a customer, all of which greatly pleases an American, and, as a result, they buy many things which they would probably not if less attention had been shown them.

After bidding adieu to Paris, which, of course, we did very reluctantly, we returned to London, remaining there a few days, and then pushed on to Glasgow and Greenock, from which latter place we took passage on the "Devonia" for New York, arriving there, after rather a rough voyage, on Sunday, September first. Having reached America, which I had never so fully appreciated before, I will draw this correspondence to a close.